O'BRIEN SERIES FOR YOUNG READERS

 panda cubs

 pandas

 panda legends

 flyers

Can YOU spot the sword

hidden in the story?

O'BRIEN panda legends

PANDA books are for young readers
making their own way
through books.

Finn's Thumb

Retold by
FELICITY HAYES-MCCOY

Pictures by
•Randall Stephen Hall•

THE O'BRIEN PRESS
DUBLIN

First published 2008 by The O'Brien Press Ltd,
12 Terenure Road East, Dublin 6, Ireland.
Tel: +353 1 4923333; Fax: +353 1 4922777
E-mail: books@obrien.ie
Website: www.obrien.ie

ISBN: 978-1-84717-035-4

British Library Cataloguing-in-Publication Data
Hayes-McCoy, Felicity
Finn's thumb. - (Panda tales)
1. Legends 2. Children's stories
I. Title II. Hall, Randall Stephen
823.9'2[J]

The O'Brien Press receives assistance from

the arts
council
schomhairle
ealaíon

1 2 3 4 5 6 7 8 9 10
08 09 10 11 12 13 14

Typesetting, layout, editing, design: The O'Brien Press Ltd
Printed and bound in the UK by CPI Bookmarque, Croydon, CR0 4TD

Once upon a time ...
not your time
and not my time ...

There was a boy
who lived in a cave
in a wood.

He lived there
with three wise
old women
who taught him
everything they knew.

They taught him to run
and to swim
and to hunt deer
and to sing songs.

The boy's name was **Finn**.

Finn could

run through the trees
without cracking a dry stick
under his feet
or catching his hair
on a twig.

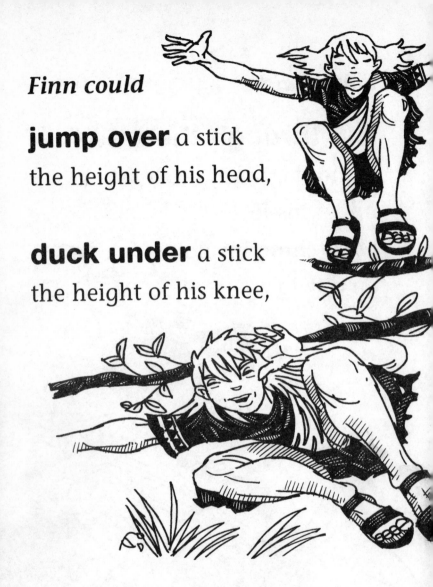

Finn could

jump over a stick
the height of his head,

duck under a stick
the height of his knee,

take a **thorn** out of his foot,
while he ran his fastest ...

... and the three old women
running after him.

He could

catch fish
and rabbits
and cook them
for dinner.

And he could take on
the three old women
at **hurling** and
beat them every time.
And crack their
hurling sticks.

So they thought
they'd taught him
enough.

And they sent him off
to find a new teacher,
who'd teach him more.

Finn walked till he came to a **field**. He walked till he came to a **stream**. He walked till he came to a **pool**.

And there was a man called **Finnegas**. He was sitting under a **nut tree**.

The tree grew by the pool.
It was very old.
Older than anything.
And very tall.
Taller than anything.
Its branches spread
over the water.

'Are you a teacher?'
said Finn.
'I am,' said Finnegas.

'Will you teach **me**?'
said Finn.

'**I might**,' said Finnegas.

'Did you ever cook a dinner?'
said Finnegas.
'I did,' said Finn.
'Right,' said Finnegas.
'You cook for me
and I'll teach you.'

So Finn stayed with Finnegas
in his house
under the nut tree.
And he cooked for him.

Now, **the nut tree's roots** reached down into the earth. Deep, deep, deep into the earth.

And they curled and twisted round **the roots of the world**.

And they made
a web of roots
deep, deep in the earth.

From the roots of the world,
the tree drew up
knowledge.

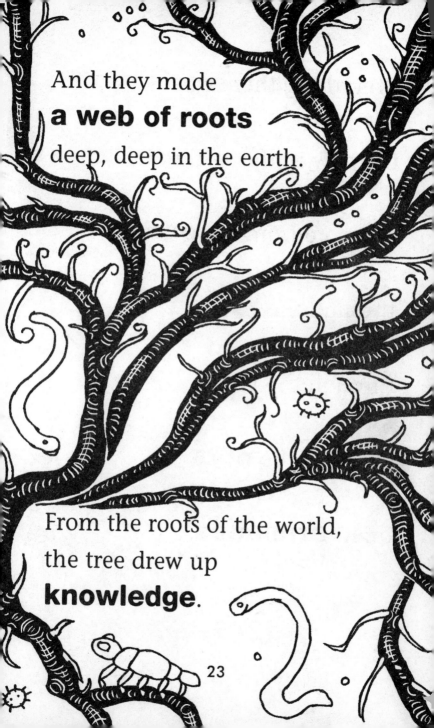

Everything there was

to know in the world

came up from the **earth**

through the **roots**

through the **tree**

and into the **nuts**

on its **branches**.

It was the
Tree of Knowledge.

Now, Finnegas
knew many things.

He knew about stars.
And he taught Finn
to name them.

He knew about numbers.

And he taught Finn
to count
and to add
and to measure.

He knew about animals.
And he taught Finn
to speak to them.

Finnegas knew many things.

But he wanted to know
everything in the world.

For hundreds of years he'd lived under the **Tree of Knowledge**.

Every year he watched the nuts ripen.

And when they were ripe
they fell into the pool.

At the bottom of the pool
lived a fish.

It was a **salmon**.

Every year
the salmon ate the nuts.
All the knowledge
of the world
was in them.

And all the knowledge
of the world
went into the salmon.

So it was the **Salmon
of Knowledge**.

One day
Finnegas spoke to Finn.
'I'll have fish today,'
he said.

He put a worm on a pin.
He tied the pin
to a thread.
He dropped it
into the pool.

And he caught
the Salmon of Knowledge.

Then he told Finn
to make a fire.

36

'Roast that fish
for my dinner,' he said.
'But don't eat any of it.'

'That's **my fish**,'
said Finnegas.
'You can't have it.'

Finn knew what to do.

The three old women
had taught him
how to rub two sticks
together
to make a spark
that made a flame
that made a **fire**.

Finnegas went off
to do something.

And Finn minded the salmon.
He kept the fire bright,
and he turned the fish.

He was hungry
but he didn't eat a bite of it.

When the salmon was done
it was roasting hot.
Finn took it off the fire.

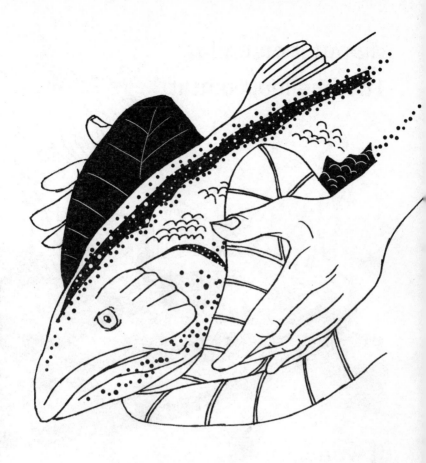

It was so hot
he used two big leaves
to lift it.

He put it on a plate.
Then he looked at it.

'I wonder is it
too hot
for Finnegas to eat?'
he said.

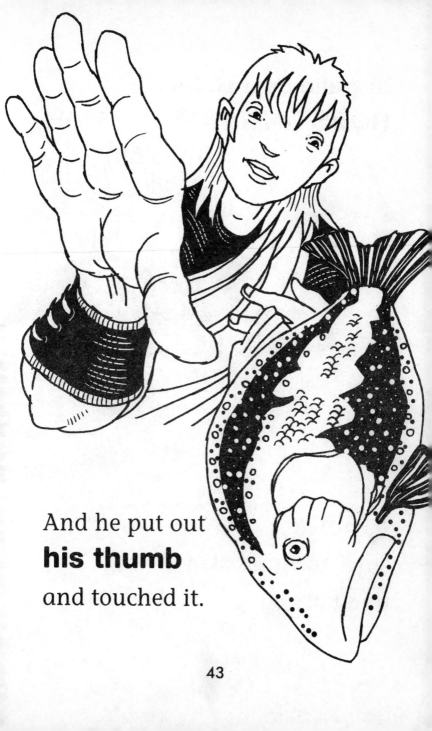

And he put out
his thumb
and touched it.

The salmon was still
ROASTING HOT.

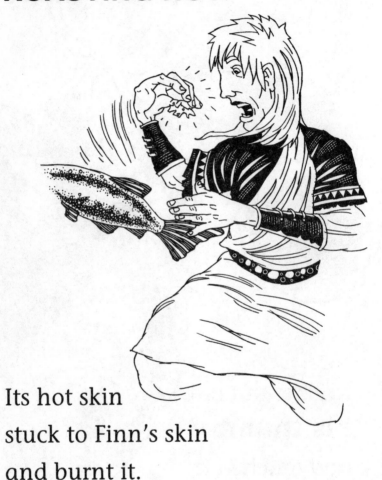

Its hot skin
stuck to Finn's skin
and burnt it.

'EEE-YEEEOWWW-EEE,'

said Finn.

And he stuck his thumb
in his mouth
to cool it.

When Finnegas
came back
he looked
at Finn.

'You've had my salmon,'
he said.
'I have not,' said Finn.
'You have,' said Finnegas.

'I have not,' said Finn.

'But I burnt my thumb on it.

And I put my thumb
in my mouth
to cool it.'

Finnegas was furious.

He kicked the fire.
He kicked the tree.
He kicked the salmon.

Finn didn't know
what was wrong.

'I'll tell you what's wrong,'
said Finnegas.

'Whoever tastes
the Salmon of Knowledge
has to eat it.
And whoever eats it
**will know everything
in the world**.'

'Oh,' said Finn.

'**You** touched it,' said Finnegas,

'I did,' said Finn.

'Then **you** put your thumb
in your mouth,'
said Finnegas.
'I did,' said Finn.

'So **you** tasted it,'
said Finnegas.

'And now **you**'ll
have to eat it,' he said.
'And **you**'ll know
everything in the world.'

'Oh,' said Finn.

Finnegas wanted to eat
the Salmon of Knowledge.
But now he couldn't.
It was **Finn** who ate it.

He ate it with
salt and butter.
It tasted fine
even though
Finnegas had
kicked it.

Then all the
**knowledge
of the world**
came into Finn's mind.

It flowed from the
earth …
through the
roots
through the
tree

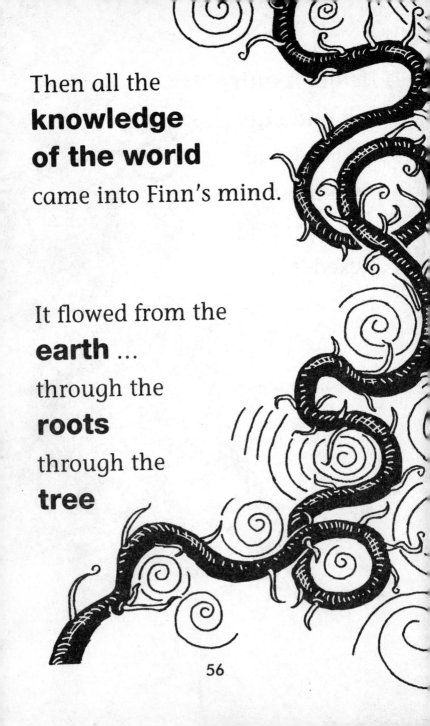

through the **branch**

through the **nuts**

through the **fish**

... into **Finn**.

And from that day on,
whenever Finn needed
to know anything,
he put his thumb
in his mouth
and he bit it.

Then he knew
what he needed to know.

But **knowledge**

never comes easy.

Finn had to bite hard.
From **tooth**
to **skin**
and from **skin**
to **bone**.
It hurt so much
that he cried.

He bit so hard
he saw stars.

But it was worth it.
Thoughts curled
and twisted
into his mind.

Each thought
twisted round another.
They made a **web**
deep, deep in his mind.

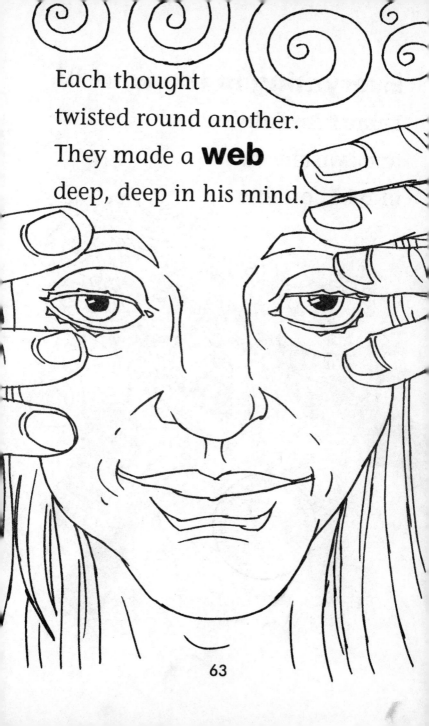

Everything in the world

came into Finn's mind
through the web
of his thoughts.

So it was worth it.